Gargoylz

Mess at the Mill

Burchett & Vogler
illustrated by Leighton Noyes

GARGOYLZ: MESS AT THE MILL

A RED FOX BOOK 978 1 849 41462 3

Published in Great Britain by Red Fox Books,
an imprint of Random House Children's Books
A Random House Company

This edition published 2011

1 3 5 7 9 10 8 6 4 2

Series created and developed by Amber Caravéo

Mixed Sources
Product group from well-managed
forests and other controlled sources
www.fsc.org Cert no. TT-COC-002139
© 1996 Forest Stewardship Council

Set in Bembo Schoolbook

Red Fox Books are published by Random House Children's Books,
61–63 Uxbridge Road, London W5 5SA

www.**kids**at**randomhouse**.co.uk
www.**totallyrandombooks**.co.uk
www.**randomhouse**.co.uk

Addresses for companies within The Random House Group Limited can be found
at: www.randomhouse.co.uk/offices.htm

THE RANDOM HOUSE GROUP Limited Reg. No. 954009

A CIP catalogue record for this book is available from the British Library.

Printed and bound in Great Britain by CPI Bookmarque, Croydon, CR0 4TD

For George Leonard Teare,
with love from great Auntie Sarah
- Burchett & Vogler

For Hugh Robb – Zack's best friend!
- Leighton Noyes

Gargoylz Fact File

Full name: Tobias the Third
Known as: Toby
Special Power: Flying
Likes: All kinds of pranks and mischief – especially playing jokes on the vicar
Dislikes: Mrs Hogsbottom, garden gnomes

Full name: Barnabas
Known as: Barney
Special Power: Making big stinks!
Likes: Cookiez
Dislikes: Being surprised by humanz

Name: Eli
Special Power: Turning into a grass snake
Likes: Sssports Day, Ssslithering

Full name: Enoch
Special Power: Doing the voices of any character he's ever read about
Likes: Exciting stories and learning new pranks
Dislikes: Loud, scary noises

Full name: Bartholomew

Known as: Bart

Special Power: Burping spiders

Likes: Being grumpy

Dislikes: Being told to cheer up

Full name: Theophilus

Known as: Theo

Special Power: Turning into a ferocious tiger (well, tabby kitten!)

Likes: Sunny spots and cosy places

Dislikes: Rain

Full name: Zackary

Known as: Zack

Special Power: Making himself invisible to humanz

Likes: Bouncing around, eating bramblz, thistlz, and anything with pricklz!

Dislikes: Keeping still

Full name: Jehieli
Known as: Jelly
Special Power: Turning to jelly
Likes: Having friendz to play with
Dislikes: Bulliez and spoilsports

Name: Ira
Special Power: Making it rain
Likes: Making humanz walk the plank
Dislikes: Being bored

Name: Cyrus
Special Power: Singing lullabies to send humanz to sleep
Likes: Fun dayz out
Dislikes: Snoring

Name: Rufus
Special Power: Turning into a skeleton
Likes: Playing spooky tricks
Dislikes: Squeezing into small spaces

Full name: Nebuchadnezzar
Known as: Neb
Special Power: Changing colour
to match his background
Likes: Snorkelling
Dislikes: Anyone treading on his tail

Name: Azzan
Special Power: Breathing fire
Likes: Surprises
Dislikes: Smoke going up his
nose and making him sneeze

Full name: Abel
Special Power: Turning into a tree
Likes: Funny puns and word jokes
Dislikes: Dogs weeing up
against him

Name: Ruben
Special Power: Can go anywhere
in the world in a blink of an eye
Likes: Mrs Santa's baking
Dislikes: Delivering Christmas presents
to houses where there aren't any snackz
for Santa and his reindeer

School Report - Max Black

Days absent: 2

Days late: 5

Max is never afraid to make a contribution to history lessons. His demonstration of a battering ram using a broom and a bucket was very realistic, although the resulting hole in the classroom door was not ideal.

I worry that Max only seems to play with Ben Neal, but he assures me he has a lot of friends at the local church.

Class teacher - Miss Deirdre Bleet

Max Black's behaviour this term has been outrageous. He has repeatedly broken school rule number 739: boys must not tell 'knock knock' jokes in assembly. He is still playing pranks with Ben Neal. Mrs Pumpkin is absent again after the exploding paint pot incident. And Mrs Simmer, the head dinner lady, says the mincing machine has never been the same since he fed his maths test into it.

Head teacher - Hagatha Hogsbottom (Mrs)

School Report - Ben Neal

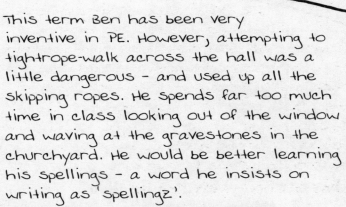

Days absent: 1

Days late: 6

This term Ben has been very inventive in PE. However, attempting to tightrope-walk across the hall was a little dangerous - and used up all the skipping ropes. He spends far too much time in class looking out of the window and waving at the gravestones in the churchyard. He would be better learning his spellings - a word he insists on writing as 'spellingz'.

Class teacher - Miss Deirdre Bleet

Ben Neal is always polite, but I am deeply concerned about his rucksack. It often looks very full - and not with school books, I am certain. It has sometimes been seen to wriggle and squirm. I suspect that he is keeping a pet in there. If so, it is outrageous and there will be trouble.

Head teacher - Hagatha Hogsbottom (Mrs)

Contents

1. Bad News
for *Spy-boy* Fans

Max Black and his best friend, Ben Neal, screeched round the corner in their imaginary spy rocket. It was Friday afternoon, and school was over for another week.

"Secret destination ahead, Agent Neal!" yelled Max, bursting through his front gate. "In ten minutes exactly we'll be at mission headquarters – my bedroom – with the TV turned on, ready for the last ever episode of *Spy-boy*."

"Perfect timing, Agent Black," said Ben

as they sprinted up Max's garden path. "I hope the gargoylz make it too."

The gargoylz were Max and Ben's amazing secret. The ugly stone creatures lived on the church next to their school – but the boys were the only humans who knew that they could come to life. Best of

all, the gargoylz liked to play tricks and have fun, just like Max and Ben.

"They'll be here," said Max. "They won't want to miss the last episode."

Ben sighed happily. "Spy-boy is the most awesome character in the history of most awesome characters."

Max reached out to ring the bell, but before he could, the front door swung open and his mother stood there, smiling.

"I've got a treat for you two!" she announced.

Max and Ben looked at each other in excitement.

"Pizza?" asked Max hopefully, dashing into the hall. "Covered in crushed crisps, chicken nuggets and baked beans?"

"With double-choc-and-toffee ice cream for afters?" exclaimed Ben, rubbing his tummy.

"Better than that," said Max's mum. "You're both going to spend the weekend with Uncle Bill!"

Max gawped at her.

"I knew you'd be pleased," she said.

"Who's Uncle Bill?" asked Ben, scratching his head.

"He's Max's great-uncle," explained Mrs Black. "Max hasn't seen him for years. He lives in the countryside, where it's really quiet and peaceful."

"I remember going there when I was little," said Max grumpily. "He lived in a boring cottage in the middle of some boring fields near a boring village. It was totally . . ."

"Boring?" suggested Ben.

"Worse than that," said Max. "It was mega–super– mega–boring!"

"Nonsense," said Mum. "You'll have fun. Ben's mum agrees with me — a bit of peace and quiet in the countryside will do you both good." She pointed to a rucksack by the front door. "I've packed your bag, Max, and we'll pick up Ben's on the way. Time to go."

Max had a terrible sinking feeling in his tummy — as if someone had pulled out the plug. This trip was going to be worse than boring — it was going to be a disaster! If they left now, they'd miss *Spy-boy*! And so would the gargoylz. "We can't go yet," he gasped. "*Spy-boy*'s going to start in a minute."

But Mrs Black wasn't listening. "We're leaving straight away," she told him firmly. "I have to be back in time to pick Jessica up from Brownies."

"But—" began Max.

Then an idea bounced into his brain. He turned to Ben and lowered his voice. "I've thought of a way we can watch *Spy-boy*." He tried to push his mum towards the kitchen. "Wouldn't you like a nice cup of tea before we go?" he asked sweetly.

"Good plan, Agent Black," whispered Ben. "That'll give us time."

"It's bound to work, Agent Neal," Max whispered back. "Mum never says no to tea."

"No," said Mum.

Max headed towards the stairs. "Er . . .
then . . . I'll just get my football," he said
quickly. "I'm not sure where it is. Ben can
help me look."

"Another good plan," muttered Ben.
"We can pretend to hunt for it and watch
the TV at the same time."

"I've packed it,"
said Mum.

"Er . . . then I'll
just get my, um . . .
pyjamas." Max
was halfway up
the stairs, Ben close
behind.

"I've packed
them too."

The boys threw
each other a
panicky look. They couldn't miss the last
ever episode!

"What about your special supercharged

anti-carsickness socks?" said Ben with a wink.

"Yes!" cried Max. "I can't travel without them."

"But you don't get carsick," said Mum.

"Not when I'm wearing my special socks," said Max earnestly. "I know they're in my bedroom somewhere. We'll go and find them."

"Hurry up, then," sighed Mrs Black. The boys zoomed upstairs and raced into Max's bedroom.

"Make lots of noise," said Max. "Then Mum will think we're searching. I'll put the telly on."

Ben picked up the waste bin and bashed it against the wardrobe.

"I wonder where those socks can be?" he yelled, tipping a box of dinosaurs all over the floor. Suddenly, above the crashing, they heard a chuckling, gurgling sound coming from the window. The boys spun round. Something stony was sitting on the ledge. Max's spy radar zipped into action: monkey face, big pointy ears, wings waggling in excitement. He knew what that meant. It was Toby – codename: Gargoyle Friend.

"Dangling drainpipes!" Toby exclaimed in his growly voice. "Let us in – we don't want to miss *Spy-boy*."

Max opened his window wide. Toby
flew in, snatched the TV remote and
started flicking through the channels. Three
more stone-coloured
creatures scampered over
the sill.

A big, ugly gargoyle
jumped onto the bed.
"Hello, boys," he said,
beaming all over his
warty face. "What's
the matter, Ben? Why
are you throwing
Max's shoes against
the wall?"

"Hi, Rufus," called Ben. "It's so we can
watch *Spy-boy*."

"That's a funny way to watch *Spy-boy*,"
said Jelly, flapping his pterodactyl wings.
"You're making so much noise we won't
be able to hear it."

"No – you don't understand," said Max.

"It's just that—"

A stony hand tugged at his shorts. Barney stood there, an eager look on his doggy face. "We've brought cookiez."

Pop! Zack suddenly appeared out of thin air. "Got them from the vicar's

kitchen!" he told Max. "Used special power . . . pinched them . . . right under his nose."

Each gargoyle had a secret power: Zack could make himself invisible, which was very useful for playing tricks.

"That's lovely," said Ben, "but—"

"And we've got a jolly surprise for you,"
Jelly interrupted him.

"We haven't got time for jolly surprises,"
groaned Max.

"Yooou haven't got time for *me*?" came
a solemn voice from the window. An
owly gargoyle was perched on the ledge,
peering at the boys shyly.

"Enoch!" cried Ben, forgetting their problem for a moment.

"Welcome to my bedroom," said Max in delight.

Enoch didn't live on the church roof with the other gargoylz. He lived in a big library in the nearby town, and the boys always visited him when they borrowed books. But this was the first time Enoch

had left the library to come and see them!

"Enoch's never watched TV before," chirped Toby.

"He's normally too scared to leave the library," explained Barney, handing out the cookies from a big paper bag.

"But I had to see *Spy-boy*," hooted Enoch, the tufts on his ears standing up in excitement. "Yooou know that the *Spy-boy* books are my favourites." The serious little gargoyle fluffed up his feathers and spoke in a brave, clear voice which was nothing like his own. "*This will be my*

best mission yet, Spy-boy fans!"

"Wow! That's just how Spy-boy speaks on the telly," Ben told him as he settled down on the bed with the gargoylz. "And how he speaks in my head when I read the books."

"Your secret power's great, Enoch," declared Max. "When you do characters, they really come to life."

"Shhh!" hissed Zack, shaking his mane impatiently. "Less talk, more *Spy-boy!*"

"Turn the sound up, Toby," urged Rufus.

"It's just about to start!" squeaked Jelly, bouncing on Max's pillow. "Jolly good."

"Max!" The gargoylz froze as Mrs
Black yelled up the stairs. "Surely you've
found your socks by now?"

Max and Ben looked at each other in
horror. They'd forgotten all about going
away for the weekend!

Max ran to his bedroom door. "Not
yet!" he called down, then turned back and
whispered, "Quick, Ben! Bang the drawers.
Make it sound like we're still searching."

There was a crash of drums from the
television and the words SPY-BOY burst
onto the screen. But as the boys turned

to watch, the bedroom door was flung open. Just in time, the gargoylz dived into the wardrobe. Max and Ben leaped up in panic and flung themselves in front of the television.

But it was too late.

"I might have known!" said Mrs Black crossly as she spotted Spy-boy whizzing across the screen. "The socks were just an excuse." She picked up the remote control and – *click!* – Spy-boy was gone. "Come down at once." And she stormed off down the stairs.

"Where are yoooou going?" asked Enoch as the gargoylz crept out of their hiding place.

"I've been trying to tell you," said Max grumpily. "We've got to visit my old uncle, and we have to leave right now."

Six little stony faces fell in disappointment. Then Barney put up a paw. "If we're very quiet, can we stay here and watch *Spy-boy* when you're gone?"

"Spluttering gutterz, that's a brilliant idea," said Toby, spitting cookie crumbs all over the carpet. "We promise we won't make a mess."

"Oh, all right then," said Max, feeling even more grumpy.

"Couldn't we watch a few minutes

too . . . ?" suggested Ben.

Toby pressed the remote, and Spy-boy, in his shiny blue flying suit, reappeared, roaring along on his supersonic spy-bike.

"BOYS!" bellowed Max's mother. "Come NOW."

Max and Ben sighed, tore themselves away from the television and tramped miserably off down the stairs. Mrs Black was in the hall, shaking the car keys impatiently.

From the back seat of the car, Max gazed wistfully up at his bedroom window. "*Spy-boy* must be really good," he said sadly. "The gargoylz aren't even bothering to wave us off."

Max and Ben
sat miserably
watching the
fields whizz
by. Heavy rain
battered against the
windscreen and the
countryside looked bleak.

"You're very quiet, boys," said Mrs
Black. "Tell you what, I'll put on a story
CD. I know there's one here somewhere."

There was a click. "*Welcome to Pixieland*,"
trilled a ghastly, shrill voice from the
speaker. "*In story one, our little woodland
chums start with a happy, skipping song . . .*"

"It's Jessica's favourite," said Mum.

The boys groaned.

"This is awful," hissed Ben in Max's ear.
"It's making me feel sick. I wish we really
did have supercharged anti-carsickness
socks."

"So do I," muttered Max. "I'd stuff them in my ears."

"We're missing *Spy-boy* for *this*," said Ben miserably. "The gargoylz will have seen the whole episode by now. They'll know if Spy-boy escapes from the Iron Claw and finds the Giant Magnet of Doom."

As he spoke, a dreadful smell filled the car, followed by muffled, growly giggles.

"Phwoah!" gasped Mrs Black. She quickly wound down the window. "I don't know who did that, but stop it right now!"

Holding his nose, Max nudged Ben in excitement. "Only Barney's special power could make a stink like that," he whispered, his eyes dancing with delight.

"Which means the gargoylz have missed *Spy-boy* to come with us." Ben's eyes gleamed as he fanned the smell away.

21

Max grinned. "Maybe this weekend won't be so bad after all."

The car started to bump down a narrow track, then came to a halt outside a small ivy-covered cottage that stood on its own, surrounded by trees. Max and Ben grabbed their bags and ran through the rain to the heavy wooden door with its rusty old knocker.

The door opened. Max activated his spy radar: creased trousers, thick spectacles, messy grey hair. He knew who this must be. It was Uncle Bill, codename: Boring Old Relative. He wore a faded blue pullover with holes in the elbows, and peered at Mrs Black over his spectacles.

"Hello, Joanne dear," he said vaguely.

He gave her a peck on the cheek and looked down at the boys. "Who are these two?"

"It's Max and Ben, Uncle Bill," said Mum brightly. "You know, my son and his best friend. You invited them to stay for the weekend, remember?"

"Of course, of course," mumbled the old man. "Come in. Would you like a cup of tea, dear?"

"No thanks," said Mrs Black. "I can't stop."

"Or a sandwich . . . ?" Uncle Bill went on. "I think I've got some old bread that hasn't quite gone mouldy yet."

The boys gave each other a horrified

look, and Max's mum edged towards the front door. "Er, I really have to be off, Uncle Bill," she said hurriedly. "I don't want to get stuck in traffic. Bye, boys."

Her car was soon bumping back down the rough track.

"I hope the gargoylz managed to get out of the car in time," Max whispered to Ben. "Mum left in a bit of a hurry."

"I don't blame her," Ben replied. "I wish *we* could."

"Go into the lounge and make yourselves comfy on the couch while I get

us a snack," Uncle Bill called as he shuffled slowly towards the kitchen. "I've got to watch my favourite programme on TV."

"We'd better not eat anything Uncle Bill gives us," said Ben in a low voice. "We'll get food poisoning!"

They went into the lounge and plonked themselves down on the shabby sofa.

"What do you reckon his favourite programme is?" asked Ben. "*Turnips Roadshow?*"

"Tortoise Racing?" suggested Max.

"*Tea Cosies Through the Ages?*" Ben giggled.

The door opened, and Uncle Bill strolled into the room.

But to the boys' astonishment he looked completely different. He had a lively gleam in his eyes and a broad smile on his face.

"Now your mum's gone we can have fun!" he said brightly. "I've got something special for you to do tomorrow. But for now – I hope you're both hungry."

He was carrying a tray covered in big fluffy muffins, double-iced cupcakes and glasses of sparkling lemonade. The boys peered suspiciously at the goodies.

"Don't worry," chuckled Max's uncle. "They're quite fresh! I made them today."

"So you just said all that about the bread so Mum wouldn't stay too long?" Max asked, staring up at him.

Uncle Bill winked at him. "Would I do such a thing?" he said. "Now, tuck in!"

Max and Ben didn't need to be told twice!

"These are awesome!" gasped Max as he licked the icing off his fingers.

"Thank you," said Uncle Bill. "I thought you'd like them." He aimed the remote control at the screen. "Now I'll put on my programme. I recorded it earlier. I hope you don't mind watching it."

"Prepare for mega-boredom," muttered Ben.

There was a crash of drums from the television.

Max and Ben had heard that noise before!

"It's *Spy-boy!*" cried Max in delight

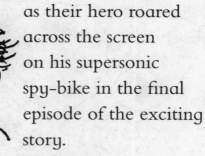

as their hero roared across the screen on his supersonic spy-bike in the final episode of the exciting story.

"This is our favourite programme too!" yelled Ben.

Uncle Bill passed him more cakes. "I can see that the three of us are going to get along just fine," he chuckled.

They all leaned back against the cushions, watching as Spy-boy was captured by the evil Hookman, thrown off a mountain, attacked by a man-eating whale and locked in the mighty Tower of Terrors.

"Shame the gargoylz can't see this," Max murmured to Ben. "It's awesome!"

There was a faint *tap-tap* at the window.

Uncle Bill was glued to the screen and didn't seem to have heard. The boys turned to see six stone faces grinning at them over the sill.

Toby held up a note.

"Spluttering gutterz!" the boys read.

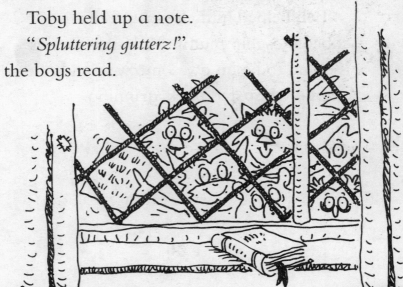

"*We haven't had so much fun since Zack made the vicar's cupcakes dance all over the table and he thought there was an earthquake.*"

Max gave the gargoylz a secret thumbs-up. "I'm glad they're not missing *Spy-boy*," he whispered happily to Ben.

Ben helped himself to his fifth chocolate-chip muffin. "It looks like this is going to be an awesome weekend after all," he whispered back, grinning.

2. The Haunted Windmill

The next morning Max opened his eyes and looked around. For a moment he couldn't think where he was. This wasn't his bedroom. The ceiling was low, with big brown beams, and there were brand-new *Spy-boy* posters all over the whitewashed walls. The sun was streaming in through the window and he could hear loud snoring from the next bed. Then he remembered!

"Wake up, Ben!" he yelled, lobbing a pillow at his friend. "Uncle Bill said we're going to do something special today!"

Ben sat bolt upright and sniffed the air. "My super-spy senses can smell chocolate, Agent Black," he exclaimed.

"We must investigate, Agent Neal," declared Max, making for the door. "My tummy's rumbling like a volcano."

"Greetingz, boyz." Toby's grinning face appeared at the open window. "You're in for a treat. We were asleep on the roof when we heard Uncle Bill clattering about in the kitchen. He's made a huge pile of cookiez!"

The boys
heard a loud
chomping in the branches
of a nearby tree. Barney's
face popped out. It was
covered in crumbs. "I'm just
having a little taste," he said,
with his mouth full, "and I have
to say, they're delicious."

"You'd better hurry or there'll
be none left, boyz," advised Toby.
"You know how much Barney loves
cookiez."

The boys thundered down the wooden
stairs and burst into the kitchen. Uncle Bill
was at the table, pouring orange juice into
two glasses. There was a big cardboard box
next to him.

"Good morning, lads!" he greeted them.
"I hope you're hungry. I've got something
special for your breakfast." He flung open

33

the lid of the box, then scratched his head, puzzled. "That's funny. I'm sure there was a whole box full of cookies when I last looked. I must have been dreaming . . ." He passed the box to Max and Ben. A few cookies lay in the bottom with a pile of crumbs.

"They're in my tummy," came a gargoyle voice from under the table.

Uncle Bill looked at Max in surprise. "They're in your tummy?"

"No," Max said quickly. "I said they . . . um . . . look yummy. And here's my favourite — with loads of chocolate chips!"

"I'll have this chewy toffee one," added Ben. "Thanks, Uncle Bill."

The two boys tucked into their delicious breakfast.

"This is the most awesome breakfast in the history of most awesome breakfasts!" Max told his uncle. "These cookies are scrummy."

Uncle Bill looked pleased. "I knew you'd like them," he said. "I made them this morning. I bake cookies every day — but usually up at the Old Mill Bakery next to the windmill. I work there, you see."

He pointed out of the window.

There was a small hill behind the cottage. An old-fashioned shop with little diamond-shaped windows stood on the top; beyond it the boys could see a magnificent white windmill, its sails moving slowly in the breeze.

"Whoa! We didn't see that last night," gasped Max. "It's awesome."

"I've never seen a real windmill before!" exclaimed Ben.

Uncle Bill turned away from the window. The boys were surprised to see that he looked sad. "It won't be there much longer," he told them. "It's stood on that site for three hundred years, grinding wheat into flour.  The flour's used in the bakery to make bread and cakes and cookies for the whole town, but the mill and the bakery are about to be bulldozed to the ground."

"That's terrible!" said Max indignantly. "Who's knocking it down?"

"A woman called Rosie Pink." Uncle Bill frowned. "She's going to build a shopping centre there instead. The top of the hill is an ideal place, she says. Everyone will be able to see it for miles around."

"A shopping centre!" Ben was disgusted.

"It's going to be called Glitter World,"

Uncle Bill went on, "and it's just for girls."

The boys' mouths dropped open in utter horror.

"It'll be all fluffy and sparkly," groaned Max.

"With stupid dolls and stinky perfume," added Ben.

Max shuddered. "And loads of girls running about shrieking!"

"Every day you'll open your curtains and see Glitter World, Uncle Bill," said Ben. "You'll have to wear really dark glasses."

Max's uncle sighed. "I wish Rosie Pink would choose somewhere else to build it.

But the windmill is owned by the council, and she got them to agree to sell it to her."

"If only Spy-boy was here," exclaimed Max. "He'd soon stop her with his super-sticky zapper."

"Or tie her up with his super-stun string," said Ben.

"Or blow her away with his super-turbo hurricane blaster," added Uncle Bill. "But I'm afraid that next week the bakery and mill are going to disappear for ever, and there's nothing we can do." He looked at Max and Ben's dejected faces. "Now, I don't want to upset you two with my problems. I'm going to make sure you enjoy your weekend here. You can explore the old mill while it's still standing."

"That will be brilliant!" cried Max.

There was a muffled "Hurray!" from inside a cupboard. Uncle Bill looked

puzzled. "Did you hear that?" he asked.

The boys shook their heads, trying not to laugh. The gargoylz were as excited as they were about visiting the windmill!

Uncle Bill crouched down and flung open the cupboard door. Max and Ben held their breath. Was he going to discover the gargoylz?

"Huh. Nothing there," he said, to their relief. "Must have been mice. There are lots of them in this cottage. Now, get dressed and we'll go to the mill. After that, you can help decorate the cookies at the bakery."

The boys raced up to their bedroom to find Toby and Enoch sitting on the bed waiting for them. Enoch had a worried frown and his stony feathers were quivering nervously.

"What's the matter?" asked Ben.

"Enoch's not sure he wants to go to the mill," Toby told them. "You know he's scared of going to new places."

"You'll be fine." Max sat down next to the owly little gargoyle. "We'll look after you . . ."

". . . and there'll be loads of cool tricks to play," added Ben.

Enoch's face broke into a grin. "Oooh!" he hooted. "I dooo love playing coool tricks."

"Let's join the others then," chuckled Toby, and the two gargoylz scuttled out of the window.

Five minutes later, Max and Ben were marching along the path to the old mill. They could hear muffled giggling and chattering as the gargoylz scampered along beside them, keeping hidden from Uncle Bill, who was leading the way.

The old man stopped and put his ear to the long grass beside the path. "Did you hear that?" he asked.

"I didn't hear anything," said Ben, giving Max a wink.

"Nor did I," agreed Max.

Uncle Bill straightened up. "Must have been weasels," he said. "There are lots of them around here. Though I've never

heard them giggling before."

Soon they arrived at the mill. Its sails were turning slowly in the wind.

Uncle Bill took a large key out of his pocket and opened the heavy wooden door.

He looked at Max and Ben's excited faces and rubbed his hands together.

"You'll have a wonderful time exploring the lovely old mill. You'll be like Spy-boy in *Spy-boy and the Stolen Jewels* when he sneaks into the secret castle."

"Awesome!" Max peered in at the dark wooden beams and heavy machinery that was slowly grinding round.

"The sails must be making it all move," gasped Ben. "It's amazing."

"I'll be in the bakery next door," Uncle Bill told them. "I'll call you when we're ready for biscuit-decorating. You two will have the place to yourselves to explore for a while. Just be careful – keep clear of the machinery."

"Uncle Bill doesn't know it," said Max as his great-uncle plodded off towards the bakery, "but there'll be gargoyle explorers too!"

He followed Ben into a circular room, lit by a few small windows. In the middle, a metal shaft stretched from floor to ceiling, connected to a series of cogs and

levers. The shaft
was revolving
slowly, making
the cogs clunk
round.

"Just the
place for super-
spies to do some
super-spying,"
declared Ben in
delight.

"With the
gargoylz' help,
of course,"
agreed Max,
creeping round a pile of bulging sacks. "I
wonder where they are."

"Not here, that's for sure," said Ben,
checking out the heavy beams above their
heads. "We can pretend that they're enemy
agents and we're searching for them."

"Secret Mission: Find the Gargoylz,"

announced Max. "Got your super-spy jet zapper, Agent Neal?"

"At the ready, Agent Black," replied Ben, holding up his imaginary zapper as

he edged towards a flight of steep wooden steps.

They crept up to the next floor, glancing into the dark corners and whipping round to check out every nook and cranny.

"This is a really creepy place," Max murmured happily.

"No sign of the enemy agents though," said Ben.

"They must be here." Max made for the next set of stairs. "We heard them on the way. Let's see what's above."

They climbed up through a hatch into a loft-like room.

"We're at the top – and still no sign of them," Ben whispered.

"I bet they're hiding," Max replied. "They're going to jump out and scare us."

"Nothing scares superspies like us," said Ben boldly. He crept across the floor towards a pile of sacks – and suddenly yelped in fright.

"I saw a face outside!" he

48

gasped, pointing at
the window.

Max laughed.
"Very funny," he
said. "You can't
fool Agent Black."

Ben shook
his head. "I'm
not playing!" he
insisted.

"I know you're
trying to trick me,"
said Max. "There's
nothing there."

"There was,"
Ben told him. "It sort of flashed past.
Look – there it goes again!"

Max peered out of the little window
and snapped on his spy radar. Stony skin,
pointy pterosaur beak, big round eyes.
He knew what that meant. "It's Jelly!" he
cried. "He's dangling from one of the sails."

"So that's why he kept appearing and then disappearing," said Ben. "The sail's turning and he's going round with it!"

"Help!" yelled Jelly as he whooshed past the window again. "I got on for a ride and now I'm jolly well stuck!"

Max and Ben burst out laughing.

"It's not funny!" called the terrified little pterodactyl from overhead. "Get me down!"

Ben spotted a small hatch in the wall. He flung it open and the boys poked their heads out. The huge sails of the windmill were creaking round in the strong wind. Now they could see Jelly clinging

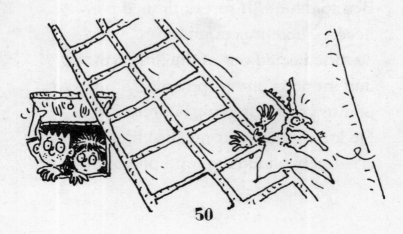

desperately to the wooden
slats of his sail.

"We've got to rescue him,"
muttered Max. "But how?"

He thrust out a hand to
catch hold of one of the little
gargoyle's wings as he went
by. But Jelly was just out
of reach.

"I've got an idea," Ben
called to the dizzy pterodactyl. "When you
come round next time, use your special
power and turn into a gloopy jelly."

"That's just what I'm trying *not* to do,"
quavered Jelly as the sail swung down
again. "I always turn to jelly when I'm
scared, but if I do it here, I'll just get
whizzed to bits. These sails are turning
faster and faster. Help!"

"If you make yourself long and
stretchy," Ben told him, "we might be able
to catch hold of you."

"Brilliant plan, Agent Neal!" exclaimed Max.

"But I'll fall off!" called Jelly in fright.

"It's your only chance," Ben called back. "You can do it, Jelly!"

The sail swung up towards their hatch, and the little gargoyle melted into a blob of purple goo. Max and Ben held out their hands as a long thin thread shot out towards them.

"Got him!" cried Ben.

They tugged as hard as they could. There was a loud slurping sound, and the ball of goo came unstuck from the sail. It flew in through the hatch, hit the boys in the

face and
knocked them
to the floor. Jelly turned
back into a gargoyle, and the
three of them rolled about on the
dusty boards, giggling helplessly.

Suddenly they heard a spooky *creak!*
They jumped up in alarm and looked
around.

"What was that?" asked Max nervously.

"I say, the mill's not haunted, is it?"
whispered Jelly, quivering with fright.

"Of course not," replied Ben, trying to
sound brave.

Crash! The hatch banged shut behind
them.

"W-w-what's happening?" wailed Jelly, jumping onto Max's head.

"I don't know," said Max. "But don't you dare turn into jelly now, Jelly! You'll get stuck in my ears!"

Woooo-oooo! came a ghostly wailing sound from above their heads. The boys froze as a flour sack rose on its own and floated through the air. Four white figures dropped down from the rafters in front of them, waving their arms eerily. A spooky mist wafted round their feet.

"Ghosts!" croaked Jelly, clinging to Max's ears. "The mill *is* haunted. Let's get out of here!"

The boys slowly inched backwards. The white figures advanced on them and the wailing grew louder. The flour sack danced around, flapping with every ghostly yowl.

Just as they reached the steps, Ben caught Max's arm. He didn't look so scared any more. "I reckon I know who

these ghosts are," he said with a grin.

"I don't care who they are," squeaked Jelly. "I'm not staying in this place another minute!"

But to Max's amazement, Ben reached

into the swirling mist and caught hold of a stony tail. A pale, wriggling gargoyle emerged.

"That's not a ghost!" breathed Max in relief. "It's Toby!"

Now they could see that the other

white figures were grinning and waving cheekily.

"And Rufus and Barney and Enoch!" exclaimed Ben.

"I knew they weren't ghosts!" declared Jelly, sliding down Max's back and giving himself a shake. "They didn't fool me."

"How did you manage to look so spooky?" Max asked them eagerly.

"Simple," said Rufus, waving his big warty arms and sending white clouds into the air. "It's flour!"

Enoch flapped his wings excitedly. "I did all the *wooooooooz!*"

"The whole thing was my idea," said Barney proudly.

"Well, it wasn't quite like that," chuckled Toby. "We sneaked into the mill after you, and Barney started looking for cookiez."

"And he accidentally fell head first into a big sack of flour—" added Rufus.

"I meant to," insisted Barney.

"And when he climbed out . . ." said Toby.

". . . he looked like a ghost!" Rufus was bouncing about in excitement.

"So we all jumped in toooo!" Enoch told them.

"And you decided to play a trick on us," said Max. "It was spooktacular!"

"Wait a minute –
where's Zack?" asked
Ben.

Pop! Zack appeared
out of thin air. "I moved
the sacks," he chirped. "Creaked the door.
Banged the hatch."

"Good haunting!" said Max in awe.

"It was amazingly creepy the way you
lot jumped down in front of us," Ben said.

Enoch blushed. "That was my idea,"
he said shyly. "I got it from my favourite
Spy-boy story – *Spy-boy and the Ghostly
Goalkeeper*."

"I remember that one!" said Max
eagerly. "Spy-boy leaps down in front
of the ghost keeper on the stadium roof.
Brilliant plan, Enoch!"

Toby beamed from ear to ear. "We
haven't had so much fun since Zack
swapped the vicar's flour for sherbet and
he made exploding muffins!"

"I *knew* the mill wasn't haunted," said
Jelly, settling down on top
of a sack of grain.

Suddenly a door
banged. Everyone
jumped and looked
at each other. Jelly
clung to Ben's leg in
terror.

"I *knew* the mill
was haunted!" he
wailed.

"Come along, boys!" came a familiar
voice from down below. "Cookie-decorat-
ing time!"

"That's no ghost," said Max with a grin.
"That's Uncle Bill."

He and Ben rushed for the stairs. "We're
on our way!" they yelled.

"I'm going to put caramel crunchies on
mine," said Ben.

"And mine are going to have triple-chocolate-fudge bits on," said Max.

"Wait for us!" called Jelly. "We want to help."

"And maybe taste some!" added Toby.

"That's right," said Barney, scurrying down the steps. "We haven't eaten a thing since breakfast!"

3. Scary Bones

Max and Ben poked their heads round
the door of the bakery kitchen, ready for
cake-decorating duty. It was a warm,
inviting room just behind the shop. Every
surface was covered with trays of delectable
goodies, hot from the oven. Their little
stony friends pushed eagerly in behind
them.

"Dangling drainpipes!" whispered Toby.
"Those cookiez smell delicious."

"Uncle Bill's stirring an enormous pot
of melted chocolate," Max whispered back,
"and I can see loads of cakes."

"Muffinz!" sighed Barney, his round eyes popping out of his stony face.

"Pastriez!" drooled Rufus.

"Tartz," gasped Jelly. "Bursting with jam."

"Scrummy-yummy, get in my tummy!" whooped Zack.

The gargoylz tiptoed across the floor and hid under the table.

"Come on in," Uncle Bill called to Max and Ben. "You're just in time to help me put the finishing touches to my latest creation. I'm calling them the multi-choc criminal cookies."

"How can a cookie be criminal?" asked Max, going over to inspect the scrumptious baking.

The old man's mouth turned down

sadly. "Because these cookies are my greatest ever invention and it's an absolute *crime* that this is the only time they'll be made and sold at the bakery."

"I don't understand," said Ben. "I thought you had another week before it closes down."

"So did I," said Uncle Bill. "But I've just had a phone call from Rosie Pink. She wants the bakery to shut today."

"That's terrible," came Toby's voice from under a chair.

"You're right, Max," said Uncle Bill.

"But you sound a bit croaky. You'd better have a drink." He passed Max a glass of milk, and pushed a bowl across the counter to the boys. It was full to the brim of all types of chocolate decorations. "I'll leave you to put the finishing touches to the multi-choc criminal cookies. I might as well start packing up the shop. Miss Pink's coming along later to make sure we're ready to leave."

He opened a door, and beyond him the boys could see into the shop. Shelves full of bread stretched around the walls, and cake boxes with a windmill design were arranged in the windows.

An old-fashioned
cash register
stood on a table
in the middle.

As soon as
Uncle Bill had
gone, the boys
and gargoylz got
into a huddle.

"I don't understand," said Ben. "How
could anyone pull down this wonderful
place of yumminess and put up Glitter
World instead?"

"It's terrible," wailed Barney. His doggy
face began to quiver. "I'm so upset I
could—"

Enoch rushed over. "No bottom burps
here," he hooted. "Yoooou will spoil the
wonderful aroma of cake. And we've got
work to dooo!"

"Enoch's right," said Max, grabbing a
handful of white chocolate drops.

"Let's decorate the cookies for Uncle Bill. At least he'll have something good to sell to his last customers."

Everyone set to work, plopping icing onto the big crunchy cookies and covering them in bright decorations.

"I'll put white choc sprinklz on them," said Rufus.

"Squirty chocolate whirlz for me!" declared Zack, picking up a tube of icing.

"Where's Jelly?" asked Ben as he piled a plate with cookies and put them on a shelf.

"Here!" came a sticky voice from a pan of melted chocolate. "Just practising my swimming!"

"And Barney's disappeared now," said Max.

There was a loud crunching sound from behind them. Barney was perched on the shelf next to the plate of cookies, happily munching his way through them. "Just making sure they're OK," he said. "The first seven were lovely."

"Look at this!" said Toby, holding out a cookie with white chocolate chips stuck all over it. "I've made a picture of Enoch."

Enoch scuttled over and inspected the shaky design. He gave a hoot of laughter. "I look more like Rooofus!"

Rufus was dipping his warty nose into a pot of caramel and drawing patterns on

his cookie. "I'm so handsome, everyone will want to buy that one," he said.

"Not so handsome at the moment," Max told him. "You've got sticky goo all over your face!"

"So have you!" cried Rufus, scooping up some caramel and flinging it at Max.

Max ducked and it hit Jelly on the beak.

"Oh, I say!" he gasped. He grabbed a clawful of choccy drops and pelted Rufus with them.

Pop! Zack suddenly appeared next to
Ben and dropped sprinkles down his neck.

Toby flew over and dive-bombed them
all with marshmallows while Barney and
Enoch squirted each other with tubes
of icing. Soon the food fight was in full
swing. The floor and walls were covered in
splodges of chocolate and caramel – and
so were Max, Ben and the gargoylz.

"*Stop!*" yelled Max. "We promised
Uncle Bill we'd help him. All we're doing is
making a mess."

"You're right," sighed Toby. "But I
haven't had so much fun since Zack

covered the vicar
with marzipan while
he was asleep and
turned him into a
Christmas cake."

"Let's get this kitchen
tidied up," said Max, wiping
caramel smears off his jumper and pulling
a marshmallow out of his ear.

"We'll help," said Barney happily as he
licked the table clean.

They were hard at work when a shrill
ting-a-ling-a-ling was heard outside.

"What was that?" demanded Ben. "It
sounds like the fairies have arrived."

Toby flew over to the window ledge.
"It's a car horn," he told them, "and the
car's all pink and sparkly. Someone's
getting out." He gave a sudden jump
and nearly fell off the ledge. "Spluttering
gutterz!" he gasped. "Who's that?"

The boys joined him, and Max put

his spy radar on full power. Long blonde hair, shiny pink suit, sharp scowling face. He knew what that meant. It was Enemy Agent Rosie Pink, codename: Windmill Destroyer!

"I hope she doesn't come in here," said Max, looking at the chocolate still dripping from the ceiling.

The two boys crawled across the floor and peeped round the door. The gargoylz followed.

"What's she carrying?" whispered Rufus, pointing to a small, growling ball of fur poking out of her handbag.

"Is it a rat? You humanz do have funny pets."

"It's a dog," Ben whispered back.

"With a pink collar that matches her suit," groaned Max.

"And a pink ribbon on its head!"

"Is it in pain?" asked Barney. "It's making a horrible noise."

The little dog was yapping shrilly at Uncle Bill as he came out to greet his visitor. He was holding his hand out, ready to shake hers.

Grrrr-ruff! The dog snarled and snapped at Uncle Bill, who jumped back just in time. Miss Pink pushed him aside and marched towards the bakery, her sparkly pink high heels clicking on the stone steps.

As she flung open the door, Max and Ben jumped hurriedly to their feet right in front of her.

Rosie Pink reeled back in shock and nearly fell off her high heels. The dog leaped out of her handbag and began to nip at Max's ankles. "You nasty boys!" screeched Miss Pink, scooping up the yapping dog and cradling it in her arms. "You've frightened Mr Miffles."

She stopped at the sight of the chocolate-covered, sprinkle-splattered kitchen. The corner of her mouth curled in disgust. "This is revolting!"

"So is her face!" came a growly voice from under the table.

Rosie Pink glared at Max. "What did you say?"

"I said it's a disgrace!" he blustered.

"I'm glad you agree," snapped Rosie Pink, tossing her head. "In fact, it's making me feel quite faint. I hope the mill doesn't look as dreadful as this inside. I demand to see it — right now."

Uncle Bill steered her out. At the door, she turned and plonked her dog down facing the boys. "Mr Miffles is going to make sure that you horrible children behave," she announced.

76

She swept out, slamming the door behind her. The moment she'd gone, Mr Miffles ran around the boys in angry circles, yapping and growling.

"What can we do?" asked Max helplessly. "If we move, he'll bite us."

"You're right," replied Ben. "He may be small, but he's got the sharpest teeth I've ever seen."

"Hold on, Agent Neal," said Max

suddenly. "I spy someone creeping up to help us."

"Zack!" exclaimed Ben in delight.

The cheeky-faced gargoyle gave them a huge wink. *Pop!* The next second he was invisible, and Mr Miffles found himself being pushed across the floor towards the kitchen by an invisible paw.

"Zack to the rescue!" declared Max, peering through the kitchen door.

He and Ben ran in to find the little dog yapping fit to burst. Rufus was standing in front of him, just out of reach. His stony friends were safely up on a high shelf.

"Did you want to bite someone?" the warty gargoyle taunted Mr Miffles. "How about this . . . ?"

And with that he used his special power and changed into a huge skeleton.

Mr Miffles's eyes lit up. He leaped at Rufus. But before he could get his teeth into the bones, the skeleton danced off around the bakery. Then it stopped and waved cheekily. The excited little dog sprang, but the skeleton skipped out of reach. Mr Miffles put his head on one side and gave a confused whine.

"He's never met dancing bones before," laughed Max.

At the sound of Max's voice, Mr Miffles whipped round. With a vicious snarl he threw himself at the boys' legs. They vaulted up onto the work table.

"He nearly bit my ankle!" gasped Ben. "We got out of trouble just in time."

Suddenly a pair of bristling ears and scrabbling paws appeared on the edge of the table.

"We're not out of trouble yet," warned Max.

A hairy face came into view, and Mr Miffles hauled himself up onto the table. Teeth bared, he began to advance through the bowls of sprinkles and nuts. The boys backed away.

"We've run out of table," whispered Ben as they wobbled on the edge. "What are we going to do?"

Max looked around in a hurry. There was a pan of caramel sauce on a nearby shelf. "Secret Plan: Caramel Roll," he hissed to Ben. "When I say 'duck', duck!" He looked around the kitchen for their stony friends. "Listen, gargoylz," he called loudly, "get that pan and put it on the floor by the table."

"Gargoylz to the rescue!" yelled Toby, launching himself into the air, while Jelly, Barney and Enoch scuttled down from their shelf.

Mr Miffles was too busy inching towards Max and Ben to notice the stony little figures placing a large bowl of gloopy caramel on the floor at the end of the table.

With a fierce growl, Mr Miffles sprang at the boys.

"Duck!" yelled Max. Max and Ben threw themselves down. A ball of furious teeth and fur sailed over their heads, off the end of the table – and *flumph!* into the caramel.

The little dog climbed out and rolled helplessly

around the floor, picking up chocolate buttons and sprinkles on his caramel-covered fur. At last he managed to struggle to his feet in a sticky daze.

The kitchen door opened and a shriek filled the air. Rosie Pink stood frozen in the doorway, with Uncle Bill behind her. "I have never seen a more disgusting cake in my life!" she screeched, pointing in horror at Mr Miffles. Max looked at Uncle Bill. He could see he was struggling to keep a straight face.

"That's not a cake," said Ben. "It's your dog."

"Mr Miffles!" Rosie Pink gasped in shock. "What have they done to you?"

"We haven't done anything," said Max truthfully. "Mr Miffles tried to attack us . . ."

"Rubbish!" snapped Rosie Pink. "Mr Miffles wouldn't attack anyone."

". . . and he accidentally fell in the caramel," finished Ben, putting on his best innocent smile. "It was just bad luck that the pan happened to be there."

She grabbed a tea towel. "Mummy's going to take you home, my little darling," she cooed as she wrapped the snarling dog in it. Holding him at arm's length, she marched to the door, where she spun round and glared at them all. "The sooner this place is demolished, the better!" she screeched. "The bulldozers will be here first thing tomorrow."

With a spray of gravel, she sped off in her car.

Uncle Bill gave a long sad sigh. "I tried to persuade her not to knock the mill down," he told the boys, "but she wouldn't listen."

"She's horrible," gasped Max.

"We haven't got much time left," sighed Uncle Bill. "I'm going to box up all the cookies you decorated. We don't want them getting bulldozed along with the bakery."

He shuffled off and began stacking the cookies. The boys went outside and stared up at the windmill, its sail still slowly turning.

"I wish we could do something," said Ben.

"So do we," said a growly voice, and the gargoylz tumbled out of a nearby bush.

"That Rosie Pink shouldn't make her dog scare people." Barney was frowning.

"She needs a good scaring herself," agreed Jelly.

As he heard those words, a brilliant idea burst into Max's brain. "That's it!" he exclaimed. "Prepare for a secret plan, everyone."

"What is it?" asked Toby eagerly.

"Tell us," demanded Rufus.

"Secret Plan: the Big Scare," Max told them. "When Miss Rosie Pink comes back tomorrow, we'll give her the fright of her life!"

4. The Big Scare

Max and Ben stood solemnly beside Uncle Bill in the Old Mill Bakery. Today was the day Rosie Pink was coming to take the keys of the mill and bakery. Today was the day they were going to be bulldozed to the ground.

A deep, deafening rumble of machinery suddenly shook the bakery as three huge yellow bulldozers lumbered up. There was an ear-splitting screech of tyres and a familiar car pulled up in front of them. Rosie Pink stepped out. She wore a glittering salmon-pink suit and had bright

pink combs in her blonde hair. Her mouth was a grim line of shiny pink lipstick.

"Yuck!" exclaimed Max. "What a horrible sight."

"She looks like a giant pink stick insect," said Ben.

Mr Miffles poked his head cautiously out of her handbag. He still had sprinkles on his nose and a chocolate button stuck to one ear.

"We'd better go and meet her!"

muttered Uncle Bill as Miss Pink marched towards the bakery in her bright pink high heels. He stopped at the door and turned to the boys. "Are you sure you want me to take her picture inside the windmill?" he asked, gazing glumly at the camera in his hand.

"Oh yes," said Max eagerly. This was stage one of their secret plan. "I bet she won't be able to resist having her photo taken."

"And you can take some extra pictures for yourself," added Ben. "Without Rosie Pink in them!"

"So that you can remember what the mill was like," Max told him.

"We really think you should," insisted Ben.

Uncle Bill stared hard at them.

"Are you two up to something?" he said, his eyes beginning to twinkle. "You look just like Spy-boy when he's on a secret mission."

"Us?" said Max innocently.

"I don't know what you mean," said Ben.

Uncle Bill chuckled. "That's just what Spy-boy would say."

They went out to meet Miss Pink, who was tapping her foot impatiently. Mr Miffles gave a growl as they approached.

"You'd better have the keys ready," she snapped.

"Come into the bakery," sighed Uncle Bill. "They're in the drawer."

Rosie Pink gave the boys a nasty scowl and swept off through the bakery door. Uncle Bill followed. As soon as the door had closed, big grins spread over the boys' faces.

"Ready for action, Agent Neal?" asked Max. "Time for Secret Plan: the Big Scare."

"Ready, Agent Black," answered Ben. "This is going to be such a cool trick. That horrible woman deserves a good scaring for wanting to turn the mill into a stupid girly shopping centre."

"And the gargoylz will do that brilliantly!" said Max. "They scared us yesterday so they're sure to scare her. I hope they're all in their places in the mill."

"Poor Uncle Bill," said Ben. "He did look sad. Our little prank is sure to cheer him up."

At that moment they heard the bakery door open and Miss Pink's shrill voice.

"I don't want my photo taken in that ghastly place!" she was snapping at Uncle Bill as she stepped outside. "And nor does Mr Miffles. Just hand over those keys and go."

"Oh no, Agent Neal!" groaned Max. "We can't carry out the plan if she won't go into the mill."

"Too right, Agent Black," agreed Ben. "We're relying on Uncle Bill."

They watched anxiously as Max's uncle edged Rosie Pink towards the mill. She was holding out a brightly nail-varnished hand for the keys.

"The local

paper's going to put the pictures on its
front page," called Max quickly.

Rosie Pink patted her hair. "Local
paper, eh?" she said. "Very well, then. Just
one photo, and then I want you gone!"

"Quick!" whispered Ben. "To the
windmill. We've got to give the gargoylz
the password. Then they'll know that she's
on her way."

Max and Ben dashed round the back
of the bakery and scooted over to a small
window in the side of the mill.

"Cookies!" hissed Ben loudly.

"*Message received loud and clear*," came a
voice that sounded just like Spy-boy.

"Good old Enoch," said Max. "Now
let's watch the fun."

"The gargoylz are well
hidden," whispered Ben.
"Wait – there's Zack just
above the door—"

Pop! Zack disappeared.

"Brilliant," hissed Max. "Now I can only see machinery and bags of flour . . . Oh no, there's Jelly running across the floor! He needs to get in position behind the sacks, but if he doesn't hurry up she'll see him."

The mill door swung open.

"What a sight!" they heard Miss Pink shriek.

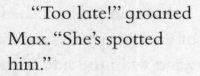

"Too late!" groaned Max. "She's spotted him."

They peered in anxiously.

But Rosie Pink wasn't gawping at a gargoyle. She was admiring herself in a sparkly pink hand mirror. "What a gorgeous sight I am!" she crooned as she stared at her reflection. "But I mustn't forget to get my little darling ready for the photo too." She pulled out a

sparkly pink brush and began to fluff up
Mr Miffles's fur.

Max heaved a huge sigh of relief. "It's
all right. She's talking to herself!"

"And she didn't see Jelly after all," said
Ben. He spotted the tip of a small purple
beak sticking out from behind the flour
sacks. "He's ready
for action."

Rosie Pink
followed Uncle
Bill inside, her
nose turned up
in disgust. The
next minute
she let out a
deafening shriek
and leaped into the
air, flapping her hands round her head.

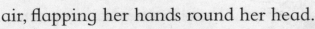

Max and Ben clapped their hands over
their mouths to stifle their giggles.

Rosie Pink glared at Uncle Bill.

"Something touched my neck!" she exclaimed.

"That must have been Zack," whispered Ben.

"It was probably just a spider," Max's uncle assured her. "There are lots of them in the mill."

Miss Pink shuddered and looked around fearfully. "Then hurry up with that photo," she said.

"Just here would be best," replied Uncle Bill. "There's plenty of light from the window."

"Be quick, then." Miss Pink checked her appearance in her mirror one last time. Then she pulled Mr Miffles out of her bag, held him up and flashed a cold smile.

Mr Miffles bared his teeth at the camera.

But as Uncle Bill got ready to take the shot, a long thin strand of purple goo appeared from behind the sacks and wiggled its way across the floor.

"Go, Jelly!" whispered Ben.

"That's so cool," Max whispered back in delight. "He's almost invisible. She hasn't seen him!"

The strand of goo wrapped itself round Miss Pink's ankles. She began to hop about, shaking her legs as if she was doing a wild dance. Quick as a flash, the Jelly goo wiggled away unnoticed.

"Something horrible slithered

around my legs," she cried. "I'm getting out of here. I told you this place was spooky."

"That was probably just a snake," said Uncle Bill soothingly. "There's lots of them around here too. Although they don't usually come inside the mill . . ."

Rosie Pink made for the door. "That was no snake. This place is haunted. I'm leaving *now*."

"Oh, but you mustn't go," said Uncle Bill quickly. "I haven't got your picture yet."

Max turned to Ben. "Time for *our* part in the plan," he said with a grin. The two boys rushed round to the mill entrance.

"Uncle Bill!" called Max. "Telephone call for you. It's urgent."

"Thanks, boys," the old man replied.

"I'll be back as soon as I can to take your photo, Miss Pink. Max and Ben will look after you while I'm gone."

"You can't leave me in this spooky place with these nasty boys!" squealed Rosie Pink, trying to dodge past Max and Ben and follow Uncle Bill out.

A dreadful creaking sound echoed around the room. Rosie Pink jumped in alarm.

"That'll be Zack wiggling the window," Max whispered to Ben.

Rosie Pink shoved Max and Ben aside and made for the door. It slammed shut in her

face and a ghostly voice suddenly filled the air.

"*I have come for yooou, Rosie Pink . . .*" it moaned eerily. "*There is no escape . . .*"

She froze to the spot, her hair standing on end. "What was that?" she croaked, clutching Mr Miffles, who started yapping in fear.

"I didn't hear anything," said Max solemnly. "Did you, Ben?"

Ben shook his
head. "I didn't
hear a thing.
I think you
should sit
down, Miss
Pink,"
he added
sympathetically.
"You don't look at all well."

Miss Pink tottered unsteadily towards
the sacks of flour.

Flumph! She'd only taken a couple of
steps when four flour-covered gargoylz
sprang down from above her head, waving
their arms. Enoch's ghostly howls filled the
room.

Rosie Pink gave a scream of terror, and
Mr Miffles dived into her handbag.

She looked wildly at Max and Ben.
"Ghosts!" she shrieked. "Ghastly howling
ghosts! Can't you see them?"

The boys
shook their heads,
pretending to be puzzled.

"*Wooo-ooo!*" cried Enoch in a terrifying voice. "*We are the ghosts of the windmill!*"

"Not for long, you creepy creatures!" quavered Rosie Pink as the ghosts of the windmill floated towards her, their big dark eyes glaring at her from their pale faces. "You'll be gone once the mill's knocked down."

"*That's what yooou think,*" Enoch went on spookily. "*But yooou are wrong. We are dooomed to stay in this place and haunt anyone who's here — whether it's a windmill or a shopping centre.*"

"Scare all the shopperz!" Zack's voice echoed round the mill. "Scare all the shopperz!"

Rosie Pink pointed a wobbly finger at the dancing gargoyle. "Surely you heard that, boys!" she demanded.

"I didn't hear anything," said Max. "Did you, Ben?"

Ben shook his head. "Not a sausage!"

Max and Ben were finding it hard not to laugh out loud. Zack, Rufus, Barney and Jelly were jumping around Rosie Pink, and Toby kept swooping at her head. All that could be seen of Mr Miffles was his quivering bottom poking out of the handbag. There was flour everywhere.

"Wait a minute," said Rosie Pink, her eyes narrowing as she stared at the gargoyle footprints in the white dusty floor.

"Uh-oh," whispered Max. "She's discovered it's a trick."

Miss Pink's mouth was curling into a cold smile. "Ghosts don't leave footpr—" She broke off and gawped in horror as one of the white figures suddenly grew into a huge skeleton in front of her eyes. It reached out a bony hand towards her and rattled its bony fingers in her face.

"*Leave this place, Rosie Pink!*" came Enoch's voice.

"*ARGGGGGHHHH!*" Miss Pink gave an ear-piercing scream and fled from the mill.

Uncle Bill came out of the bakery just in time to see Rosie Pink frantically scrabbling at her car door handle. "What's the matter, Miss Pink? Where are you going?" he asked. "I haven't taken the photo and you haven't got the keys yet."

Rosie Pink finally got the door open and jumped inside. "I don't want the keys!" she shrieked above the sound of terrified doggy yelping from her handbag. "You can keep your horrible windmill and bakery. I am never coming to this evil place again."

And she sped away, followed by the bulldozers.

Max
and Ben
looked at
each other in delight.
"Does that mean the
mill can stay open, Uncle
Bill?" asked Max.

The old man's face split into a huge
grin. "It does indeed, boys!" he cried.
"I don't know how you did it, but I do
know one thing. This calls for a celebration. How about some of those multi-choc
criminal cookies!" Humming happily, he
went into the bakery.

Max and Ben ran over to the windmill,

where six white faces were peering anxiously out of the window.

"Secret Plan: the Big Scare was a success!" cried Ben. "Your trick didn't just frighten Rosie Pink, it saved the mill too!"

The gargoylz cheered in delight.

"I thought we might need one of my smellz to get rid of her," said Barney, shaking flour off his tail. "But Rufus did the trick."

"One of your smells would have got rid of us *all*!" chuckled Max.

"Rufus, using your special power to turn into a skeleton was a brilliant idea."

"It was my best performance yet," said the warty gargoyle, taking a bow. "And Enoch did wonderful voices."

"Thank yooou!" said Enoch, fluttering an embarrassed wing.

"Scarez and shockz!" cried Zack, popping in and out of sight in his excitement. "Scarez and shockz!"

"We had a jolly good time," said Jelly, beaming with delight.

"Dangling drainpipes," declared Toby, coming to perch on Max's shoulder. "We haven't had this much fun since Zack ran around in the gardener's pyjamas and the vicar was so scared he hid up the chimney."

"This has been an awesome weekend, Agent Black," said Ben happily.

"I'm going to ask Uncle Bill if we can come again soon," agreed Max.

His uncle appeared at the bakery door and called them into the kitchen.

The cookies were piled high on plates in the middle of the table. The boys tucked in happily.

"These are the most awesome cookies  in the history of most awesome cookies," sighed Ben, licking his lips.

"If only I knew who spooked Rosie Pink," said Uncle Bill with a wink.

"I'd give them the whole lot."

"It was us!" came a growly voice.

"I *knew* it was you two," said Uncle Bill happily. "I'm sorry that you have to go home tonight, but we'll have lots of fun before you do. Help yourselves. I'm off to get you both some lemonade. It'll soothe your croaky voice, Max." And he disappeared into the shop.

Six grinning gargoylz jumped up onto the table and tucked in.

"We should call these *celebration* cookiez!" said Rufus, taking a huge bite.

"We've saved the windmill and the bakery."

"Saved the mill for Uncle Bill!" chanted Zack, skipping about.

"We can't change their name!" said Barney, shocked. "They have to be criminal cookiez."

"Why's that?" asked Max.

Barney took a cookie in each paw. "Because it would be *criminal* not to eat them," he said, cramming them into his mouth.

"Spluttering gutterz!" cried Toby. "We saw off the baddie just like Spy-boy would have done."

Max grinned from ear to ear. "It was the most awesome adventure in the history of most awesome adventures!"